"Yes," said Ahmed.

3

"Come and sit with me," said Ahmed.

Oh no!

Zab was not good

at sitting.

"Come and sing with me,"
said Ahmed.

Oh no!
Zab was not good
at singing.

"Come and stand with me,"
said Ahmed.

Oh no!
Zab was not good
at standing.

9

"Come and eat with me,"
said Ahmed.

Oh no!
Zab was not good
at eating.

"Come and draw with me,"
said Ahmed.

Oh no!
Zab was not good
at drawing.

"Come and play with me,"
said Ahmed.

Zab was very good
at playing.

15

"Wow," said the teacher.
"That was good."

17

"Thank you," said Ahmed.
"Zab helped me."

18

19

Story trail

Start

Start at the beginning of the story trail. Ask your child to retell the story in their own words, pointing to each picture in turn to recall the sequence of events.

Independent Reading

This series is designed to provide an opportunity for your child to read on their own. These notes are written for you to help your child choose a book and to read it independently.

In school, your child's teacher will often be using reading books which have been banded to support the process of learning to read. Use the book band colour your child is reading in school to help you make a good choice. *Ahmed and the New Boy* is a good choice for children reading at Yellow Band in their classroom to read independently.

The aim of independent reading is to read this book with ease, so that your child enjoys the story and relates it to their own experiences.

About the book

Zab is new at school and Ahmed is helping him to settle in. Zab is very different to the other children – in fact, he is an alien! Zab doesn't find it easy to do the some of the things that Ahmed does, but he is excellent at other things, and he ends up helping Ahmed!

Before reading

Help your child to learn how to make good choices by asking: "Why did you choose this book? Why do you think you will enjoy it?" Look at the cover together and ask: "What do you think the story will be about?" Support your child to think of what they already know about the story context. Read the title aloud and ask: "The new boy looks different to the other children. Do you think he might be an alien?" Remind your child that they can try to sound out the letters to make a word if they get stuck.

Decide together whether your child will read the story independently or read it aloud to you. When books are short, as at Yellow Band, your child may wish to do both!

During reading

If reading aloud, support your child if they hesitate or ask for help by telling the word. Remind your child of what they know and what they can do independently.

If reading to themselves, remind your child that they can come and ask for your help if stuck.

After reading

Support comprehension by asking your child to tell you about the story. Help your child think about the messages in the book that go beyond the story and ask: "Do you think that Ahmed and Zab had fun together? Why/why not?"

Give your child a chance to respond to the story: "Did you have a favourite part? Would you like an alien to come to your class? What sort of things would you do together?"

Use the story trail to encourage your child to retell the story in the right sequence, in their own words.

Extending learning

Help your child understand the story structure by using the same sentence patterns and adding some new elements. "Let's make up a new story about Ahmed and Zab having fun. In my story they go to the park. Ahmed says 'swing like me'. But Zab isn't very good at swinging. He makes the swing go too high. But Zab is very good at going round on the roundabout. He makes it go very fast. The children have great fun! Now you try. What will they do in your story?"

Your child's teacher will be talking about punctuation at Yellow Band. On a few of the pages, check your child can recognise capital letters, full stops, exclamation marks, question marks and speech marks by asking them to point these out.

Franklin Watts
First published in Great Britain in 2017
by The Watts Publishing Group

Copyright © The Watts Publishing Group 2017

Series Editors: Jackie Hamley and Melanie Palmer
Series Advisors: Dr Sue Bodman and Glen Franklin
Series Designer: Peter Scoulding

A CIP catalogue record for this book is
available from the British Library.

ISBN 978 1 4451 5463 3 (hbk)
ISBN 978 1 4451 5464 0 (pbk)
ISBN 978 1 4451 6076 4 (library ebook)

Printed in China

Franklin Watts
An imprint of
Hachette Children's Group
Part of The Watts Publishing Group
Carmelite House
50 Victoria Embankment
London EC4Y 0DZ

An Hachette UK Company
www.hachette.co.uk

www.franklinwatts.co.uk